Disney's
American Frontier #8

CALAMITY JANE
AT
FORT SANDERS
A Historical Novel

By Ron Fontes and Justine Korman
Illustrations by Charlie Shaw
Cover illustration by Dave Henderson

DISNEY PRESS

NEW YORK

Look for these other books in the
American Frontier series:

Davy Crockett and the Creek Indians

Davy Crockett and the Highwaymen

Davy Crockett and the King of the River

Davy Crockett and the Pirates at Cave-in Rock

Davy Crockett at the Alamo

Johnny Appleseed and the Planting of the West

Sacajawea and the Journey to the Pacific

FIRST EDITION

1   3   5   7   9   10   8   6   4   2

Library of Congress Catalog Card Number: 92-52976
ISBN: 1-56282-264-0/1-56282-265-9 (lib. bdg.)

Consultant: Catheryn Higdon, Librarian
Grundy County Jewett Norris Library
Trenton, Missouri

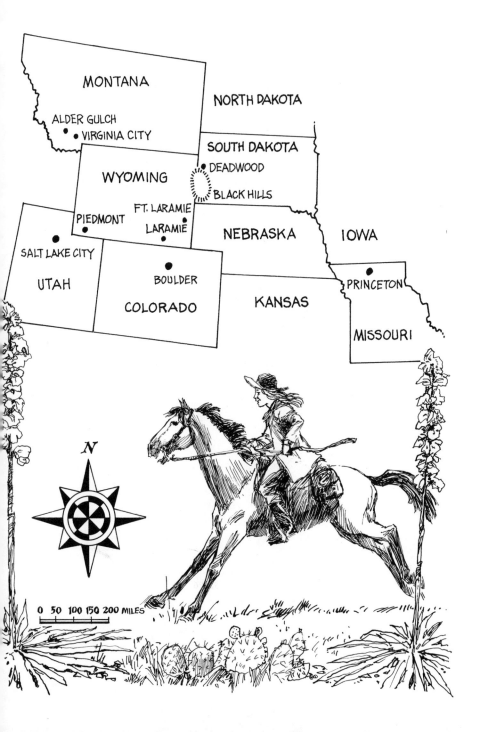

Twenty-four thundering hooves kicked up a cloud of dust down the main street of Piedmont in Wyoming Territory. Behind six sweaty horses, the fat barrel of the Overland Express stagecoach rocked and squealed on ironbound wooden wheels.

The town dogs barked at the spinning hubs. A long whip cracked, and the driver shouted to the horses in a high, shrill voice, "Wee-hah! We're comin' home!"

The hot sun poured down from the bright blue sky, baking the bustling town. Tall wooden signs shaped and painted to look like buildings covered the fronts of the stores. At a glance, these false fronts made the stores look like the grand two-story shops back in the prosperous East. But inside, most were only one small room.

Rangy cowpokes strutted past old-timers swapping lies on shady porches. Elegant ladies shopped for lace and sugar, trailing their silk gowns over the warped wooden sidewalks.

Farmers in overalls and their wives in slat bonnets and faded calico dresses loaded buckboard wagons with supplies while their children clamored for penny sweets.

The Overland Express rattled to a halt before a sagging clapboard building that served as the Piedmont Station and Post Office. The driver was a small figure wrapped in a long duster coat covering greasy buckskins, with a faded red bandanna mask to guard against the swirling dust. Fiery red hair streamed out from beneath a battered gray slouch hat.

The driver hopped off the coach almost as soon as the brakes stopped screeching and moved to catch the canvas mailbags being tossed down by the shotgun guard.

Pale-faced passengers staggered shakily from the red stagecoach. Their legs were wobbly from the jolting ride.

"Welcome to Piedmont!" the driver shouted, and then disappeared into the station stable only to return within seconds on a big black horse.

"Let's have some fun!" the driver yelled to the shotgunner. "Last one to the Silver Dollar is a no-good owlhoot!"

Then the horse and driver vanished in a cloud of dust.

"My goodness, what a young man to be driving such a dangerous route," a passenger remarked in a Boston accent. He coughed daintily into a lace-trimmed handkerchief.

The shotgunner laughed. "Aw, if weather, robbers, and wild beasts don't get you, it's a great job."

All was peaceful in the dark, cool interior of the Silver Dollar Saloon. Fancy-dressed gamblers idly shuffled cards and dice, waiting for the arrival of a new batch of stagecoach travelers. Weary cowpokes leaned against the bar, listening to greenhorn prospectors swapping brags about the gold they would find in the Black Hills of Dakota Territory.

"They'll likely find some Sioux arrows instead of gold," one cowpoke chuckled.

The other shrugged. "Wherever there's gold there'll be fools willing to chase it. At least with cowpunching you never go hungry."

At the sound of hooves clattering on wooden boards the cowpokes looked up. The saloon's double doors slammed open, and the dusty stagecoach driver rode the big black stallion right into the saloon!

Gamblers dived out of the way. Chairs flopped over, and the horse reared beside the billiards table.

"Whoa, Jim! Steady," the driver said, pulling down the red bandanna to expose an enormous grin.

The stage driver was no man, but a young woman! She was about twenty-one years old, with lively brown eyes and strong cheekbones. Her nose looked like it had been flattened in a railroad camp fight. Although she looked more plain than pretty, her skin glowed with health and high spirits.

There were no frilly bloomers or flowered calicos for this young woman. Her duster coat and stained buckskin jacket covered a worn blue flannel shirt, and she wore homespun trousers and tall, scuffed boots. A Colt revolver swung at her hip, and a big bowie knife was tucked in her belt. "I'm Martha Jane Cannary!" she shouted. "Let 'er rip!"

The bartender sighed. He was used to Jane. She always celebrated a successful stagecoach run with a wild ride through the town, and riding her big stallion into his saloon was one of her favorite stunts.

Other folks played similar tricks, but few had Jane's flair. You couldn't be in Piedmont long without knowing Jane Cannary, the wildest woman west of the Mississippi. Jim snorted and stomped restlessly.

"What a run we had, Joe!" Jane shouted to the bartender. "There must've been fifty road agents that jumped us on the road out of Salt Lake City."

"Did you whup all them robbers single-handed?" Joe asked with a sly wink. Jane was always bragging. Everyone knew she was a terrible shot. She certainly never killed anyone—unless she talked him or her to death.

"Why, no! Purvis took out one of the varmints with that ol' Henry rifle of his," Jane replied. "But I swear my pistol darn near melted, I was throwing lead so thick and fast." She grabbed a cue stick from a rack near the green billiards table.

"Throwin' bull's more like it," a cowpoke teased.

Jane ignored him. "Which one of you greenhorns thinks you can beat me at the billiards table?" Jane pointed her cue stick.

Purvis rode in on a bay mare. "I'm ready to beat you again, Jane!" The shotgun rider was a pudgy man with a huge, drooping mustache adorning his basset-hound face.

"You've never beaten me at anything, except eating!" Jane shouted. "Rack 'em up!"

The cowpokes and gamblers called out their bets as Jane and Purvis leaned over from their saddles to knock the ivory balls into pockets. The Silver Dollar rocked with laughter and jokes until a high voice chilled the air:

"What a disgrace!"

The crowd turned to see Mrs. Eulalia Beecroft frowning from the entrance of the saloon. She was the mayor's wife and one of the wealthiest women in the county. Her somber, high-collared gown had come all the way from Chicago. Its leg-o'-mutton sleeves and enormous bustle contrasted with her unnaturally slim waist, which was squeezed into a whalebone corset. A fashionable hat perched on her tightly wound hair. Eulalia would have been a handsome woman if not for her sour expression.

Mrs. Beecroft was flanked by a flock of fellow members of the Piedmont Temperance Society, all wearing their Sunday best. Many of the women balanced parasols in their lace-gloved hands.

Joe hastily hid bottles beneath the bar. "Please, ladies, it cost me a hundred dollars to replace the mirror you broke the last time you came calling. Can't you let the men drink in peace?"

Although Joe's saloon was perfectly legal, he lived in fear of the Temperance Society's constant attempts to shut him down. Many men and women who opposed the sale of whiskey were trying to outlaw all saloons.

"We're not here about whiskey this time," Mrs. Beecroft said icily. "Although we *will* close this sinful establishment soon, you mark my words. We are here to cleanse Piedmont of the worst influence ever to walk its streets—Miss Martha Jane Cannary."

Jane bowed from the saddle. "Thank you kindly."

Purvis and the cowpokes chuckled.

Mrs. Beecroft slapped her horsewhip against her dainty gloved hand. Her closest companion, Miss Prudence Meriwether, brandished a set of sheep shears.

"Piedmont is shamed by the presence of a person of the weaker sex dressed like a male and cavorting with the lowest sort of riffraff," Eulalia scolded.

"I take exception to that," Purvis growled. "I'm the best sort of riffraff."

Jane laughed and slapped a dusty thigh. "Piedmont's just a boomtown—as likely to go bust as any. I've seen 'em come and go. Now that the railroad is finished, Piedmont's gonna vanish. That corset's done cut off the air to your brain! Someone loosen that woman's stays before she pops!"

The cowpokes laughed. Eulalia's face turned crimson with righteous fury. "Piedmont is no longer a coarse den of uncivilized heathens. The Temperance Society just had a discussion with the stationmaster, and the Overland Express no longer employs you, Miss Cannary. No respectable stagecoach should have a woman driver. The Temperance Society is here to order you to leave town."

"Folks don't even know who's driving," Jane countered. "I could be a trained monkey for all they care."

"You are a vulgar hoyden," Eulalia said.

"What's that?" Jane demanded. Her fists clenched. No one called her names and got away with it. Ask any boy from Jane's hometown of Princeton, Missouri—and some of the girls, too!

"A tomboy," Prudence sniffed.

"Although perhaps that's too kind a word," Eulalia amended. "I don't know what to call a creature like you."

"While you're thinkin' up fancy words, come up with one for yourself," Jane challenged.

Eulalia raised her horsewhip and smacked Jim's glossy black flanks. Jim bucked and snorted, and Jane landed on the billiards table, scattering balls with a clatter.

Jane jumped to her feet. "You have no argument with my horse, and I suggest you leave Jim out of this or I'll be doing some whipping myself."

"If you behave like a man, then you will look like a man!" Eulalia snapped.

Prudence grabbed Jane's shaggy red mane and raised the large, sharp shears.

Jane twisted out of the woman's grip and drew her pistol. "Nobody tells me what to do! And *nobody* cuts my hair!"

Eulalia blanched, staring at the cold blue steel of Jane's Colt. One of her companions swooned to the sawdust-covered floor, but Eulalia stood her ground. Prudence hiked her skirt and ran out of the saloon.

Jane's voice was low and menacing. "Seems like the minute a place fills up, civilization follows. I ain't got fine manners like you 'cause I was raised on hard work and hard times. My daddy, God rest him, was a dirt farmer. And my momma was a laundress. They died and left me alone in this world when I was fifteen. I've driven bull trains and been a cook. I worked the railroads and did just about anything else a man can do—and did it better! So don't you go telling me what a woman *ought* to be. This is 1873! There are women teachers, doctors, lawyers, and newspaper writers. If I wanted to be a psalm-singin', prissy, do-nothin', bustle-wearing fuss-budget, I'd move to Boston. This here's Wyoming Territory. As a female person, I can vote and hold public office. Why, I could run for president....Maybe I will!"

The Silver Dollar roared with laughter. Everything Jane said was true, but the idea of a woman president seemed ridiculous.

Jane was furious. She never could understand why women and girls were supposed to shut themselves up in a house all day acting like they were made of china.

Before the laughter died down, Sheriff Callahan, with Prudence right behind him, shouldered his way through the swinging doors and parted the flock of Temperance Society ladies. The sheriff was a big man with a bristling black beard and blue eyes that had seen too much. A silver star pierced the rough cowhide of his vest.

Callahan took Jane's pistol in his meaty hand.

"Now, Jane, we've put up with your rowdy habits for a long time," he rumbled. "But I've got me a court order here, filed by Mrs. Beecroft, says you've got to leave town."

Jane squawked, angry as a wet hen. "Now, Sheriff—"

Callahan shook his head and interrupted. "Here you are creating a public disturbance, bringing a horse into a saloon and menacing a citizen with a firearm."

Jane blushed. "Shucks, Sheriff, it ain't loaded. I haven't had any bullets since that shooting contest last Christmas."

The cowpokes laughed.

Callahan opened the Colt's cylinder and looked at the empty chambers. "You might want to clean this rust bucket if you ever *do* want to shoot it." He handed Jane her pistol. "We don't want any trouble, Jane. Best you move on."

Jane sighed. "Well, I guess I'll leave town." She faced Eulalia. "Since the sheriff ain't my brother-in-law, I can't make the law or have people fired." Jane addressed the saloon at large. "And you can all die of boredom for all I care. This town's got too many rules. I'm goin' where there ain't no fences."

CHAPTER 2

I'll miss you, Jane," Purvis said.

Jane finished packing her saddlebags, loaded down with provisions bought with the last coins of her Overland Express pay. The stationmaster hadn't been able to look Jane in the eye. He just stood there biting his mustache when Jane gave him what for. Piedmont had come to a very sorry state, Jane decided, when a good man like the stationmaster wasn't allowed to make up his own mind about whom to hire and whom to fire.

Purvis pressed a handful of bullets into Jane's callused palm. "Take care," he said. "Don't forget to load that Colt. A woman alone—"

"Is just as well-off as a man and twice as smart," Jane finished for him. But she felt a lump in her throat. Purvis was a good shotgunner and a good friend.

Jane hurtled herself into Jim's saddle and rode down the main street of Piedmont. She let out a defiant whoop that echoed between the cramped buildings.

Eulalia Beecroft's thin lips curled in a tight, triumphant smile.

Jane shouted, "Don't get your bloomers in a bunch, you old lemon! I'm as gone as last year's snow."

Jane spurred Jim into a gallop and left Piedmont in a swirl of dust. Ahead of her stretched the wide, lonely plains. Piedmont dwindled in the distance until it vanished.

Jane wasn't happy to be saying good-bye to the steady money of the stagecoach job. But she'd always known it couldn't last forever, what with the railroad puffing west on its shiny new tracks. The stagecoach would soon go the way of the pony express.

Jane kept sight of the railroad tracks to the south. As long as she stayed near the tracks, there was bound to be a town and maybe some work.

Times were hard in this part of the country, and jobs were scarce. Farms had been wiped out by drought and dust storms. Black clouds of hungry grasshoppers had swooped down to devour whole fields. Jane didn't know if the grasshoppers had come because of the drought or if they just showed up to pile troubles on trouble, for that seemed to be the way life worked.

A dry, hot wind rushed over the prairie grass, fanning it into rustling waves of pale green and gold. Jane stopped long enough to sip warm water from her battered canteen.

"Nobody tells *you* where to roll," Jane grumbled at a loose clump of sagebrush tumbling across the flat, arid land.

She scowled at a cautious prairie dog stretching up to sniff the breeze. Jane could just make out an entrance to an underground prairie dog town. She gave a wild whoop. The sleek little animal whistled a warning and disappeared into the hole. Jane never did like prairie dogs. They were too much like city folks, living all crammed together, afraid of anything new.

Folks had a way of hating anything or anyone that was different. Jane knew that from long, hard experience.

Between 1861 and 1865, during the Civil War, the church ladies and do-gooders back in Princeton, Missouri, had accused the Cannarys of being Southern sympathizers. Jane's parents, Charlotte and Bob Cannary, didn't give a hoot who won that war. But those respectable people found Charlotte a mite too wild, and Jane knew that was the real reason they wanted the Cannarys to leave.

Folks just couldn't stand that Charlotte Cannary wore flashy dresses, rode around by herself, and laughed too loud for a lady. Jane's mother didn't care what people said about her—which made them the maddest of all.

But when Jane was twelve, the Cannarys picked up and moved on. Jane grew up on the westward trail and in some of the roughest mining camps of the frontier.

Jane had crossed Wyoming Territory twice as a child. The Cannarys rode through on the Oregon Trail and the California Trail to Salt Lake City in Utah Territory in 1865 and back up through the high, dry country again on their way to Virginia City in Montana Territory.

Lots of people passed through Wyoming Territory, on their way west. Some were searching for gold, and others were running away from the war or some private troubles of their own. Jane remembered the chilling sight of many nameless graves along the trail and the bleached bones of long-dead oxen appearing in the wake of the whirling dust.

In Virginia City, at the height of the gold rush, the

Cannarys were miserably poor. Not every prospector struck gold. Jane and her little brother, Elijah, and sister, Lena, often had to beg for pennies on the street.

The only thing that kept the family going was Charlotte's work in the laundry. The Cannarys wound up in Alder Gulch, Montana, where Bob died in 1866. Charlotte lasted only a year after that.

Sweat trickled over the brim of Jane's hat onto her flushed forehead. She led Jim to a nearby cluster of cottonwood trees—the only shade they were going to get. The stubby trees huddled around a sluggish creek.

Jane dropped from the saddle to fill her canteen. "Best take a breather, Jim," she said. The big horse seemed to understand, nodding his long black neck before nibbling at a clump of curly buffalo grass.

Jane chewed on a salty hardtack biscuit and decided that satisfying her hunger wasn't the same as eating. She patted the Colt revolver. Maybe she'd use Purvis's bullets to bring in something better to eat before the day was through.

After lunch, Jane rode on. The open spaces made her feel better. She soon forgot all about Eulalia and the Temperance Society.

Jane felt at home in this wild country. Like herself, it was too free and proud to please most folks.

All of a sudden Jane noticed a party of Cheyenne braves watching her from a hilltop. She had no idea how long they had been there or where they had come from or, most important, whether their intentions were peaceful.

The Cheyennes had been mighty stirred up the past few years. The Union Pacific railroad had pushed deep into their

homeland, and the U.S. Army had built forts on their sacred ground.

Since the Civil War, the cavalry and various tribes had clashed frequently because of such disputes over land. During the previous year, the Oglala Sioux chief Red Cloud had agreed to move his tribe to a reservation. Once they settled on protected government land, things had settled down.

But not all the Sioux tribes had agreed to live on reservations. The Hunkpapa Sioux chief Sitting Bull and Crazy Horse, an Oglala Sioux, were still determined to roam free and keep the settlers off their land around the Powder River in Wyoming Territory.

Jane understood why the Sioux were mad. She didn't like being fenced in, either. She'd heard that the tribes on the reservations were given rotten beef and grain teeming with weevils. Many of the Sioux left the reservations to join those still fighting.

Jane was relieved when the Cheyennes let her just ride by. They were probably looking for dinner, too, she thought. Then she saw regular white puffs of steam rising from the south. A train sped along, the engine pulling its red and yellow cars.

The Cheyennes watched the iron horse roar and smoke its way across the plains. Jane wondered if they knew this strange machine was pulling the country into the future as surely as hunters were shooting the buffalo out of existence.

After Jane watched the train pass, she saw a couple of gray-speckled prairie hens scuttling through the tall grass, pecking at grasshoppers. But she decided not to waste any bullets on one of the fat birds. They were too hard to hit and too much trouble to pluck if she did.

Before long, Jane caught sight of two tall black-tipped ears poking above the waving grasses. She grinned. Jackrabbits made good eating.

Jane stopped Jim with a quiet "Whoa" and slid silently to the ground. The jackrabbit's ears swiveled and its gray hind legs pumped in a series of quick leaps that propelled the animal across the dusty ground at an amazing rate.

Jane tracked the jackrabbit, trying to hold her pistol steady. She fired, and the heavy revolver kicked, its thundering report rolling over the plains. The jackrabbit veered left and zigzagged all over the prairie. "Darn!" Jane muttered, and lit out after the varmint.

"Take that, ya long-eared fleabag!" Jane shouted at the flashing white tail striped with black. She fired again and again. Puffs of dust sprang up where the lead slugs struck the dry ground. Squeezing off her last bullet, Jane saw the furry body fall. She ran to pick up her prize.

Cottonwood trees were too green to burn, so Jane gathered buffalo chips to build a fire. She skinned the rabbit and fried up a mess of beans in her blackened iron skillet.

Soon, roasting rabbit hissed on a spit above the fire. Jane looked away from the smoke to see the orange sun dip behind the blue mountains.

The jackrabbit was a bit stringy, and greasy, too. But to Jane, it tasted mighty fine with the red beans.

Jane smiled at Jim, who was now happily munching grass beside her. At least the company couldn't be beat, she thought.

Eulalia could keep the restaurants and starched linen tablecloths. Jane had never known a fancy meal to compare with one cooked out in the open.

The sky turned a mellow gold, and the air grew colder with each passing moment. Jane took down her blanket and spread it near the fire. She stretched out and watched sparks float up from the fire to greet the stars appearing in the dark blue sky.

Jane swatted at the pesky mosquitos and snuggled into her blankets. Nights were always cold out on the plains, but somehow the mosquitos never seemed to mind.

A big orange moon eased between the mountain peaks, soon losing its ruddy glow to shine like a silver coin. A lone coyote howled at the Man in the Moon. Jane howled back. This was heaven—but not the one Eulalia sang about in her psalms. This was a bliss city folk could never know.

The next several days blended together in a haze of heat and boredom as Jane bounced along in Jim's saddle. The dusty miles blurred beneath his steady hooves.

After she had eaten almost all of her canned beans and was cussing that darn jackrabbit for using up all her bullets, Jane started to wonder where her next meal would come from.

As Jim lurched along, Jane dozed in the saddle. At first she thought she was dreaming when she heard music. Then she blinked her eyes open. She still heard a bugle's tinny call. Jane rubbed the dust from her eyes and spied a bright flag fluttering above a tiny cluster of buildings on a distant rise. Heat shimmers made the fort seem like a mirage.

Jane whooped, "Our starvin' days are over, Jim!" Right then and there, Jane knew what she would do—become a scout!

She had always thought that scouts like Jim Bridger, Kit Carson, and Buffalo Bill Cody were the soul of the cavalry.

The army tactics of the time worked fine on Civil War battle-fields, where men lined up and shot at each other in tidy lines. But the officers, baffled by the hit-and-run tactics of some tribes, often relied on scouts.

Scouts knew tribal ways and the best paths through dangerous country. They led troops and supply wagons to lonely outposts and helped the army find new railroad routes.

Scouts were respected because of their great knowledge of the woods. Some were full-blooded Arapahos, Cheyennes, or Crows. Many were part Sioux or part Blackfoot. Still others were mountain men like Jim Bridger, wilderness-hardened trappers and hunters who had learned the ways of the woods and hills.

Although they worked for the army, scouts managed to avoid its stiff rules and regulations. They didn't have to wear uniforms, and if a scout got restless, he could simply move on. When a soldier signed up, he had to stay and do his duty.

This is perfect for me, Jane thought. Scouts don't even have to tell the army much of anything about themselves.

"Not a good enough woman, am I? Well, all right!" Jane told Jim. "I'll be a man!"

Jane pinned her long hair under her hat. "Hmm...now all's I need is a proper scout name. Martha Jane Cannary never did have much spunk. Wild Bill's great, but it's already taken. Silent Sam...Slim...hmm...those won't work, either. Maybe I could be from somewhere special, like California Carl....Nah, I haven't been there yet." Jane grinned at her horse. "Missouri Jim! You don't mind if I borrow your name, do you?"

Jim whinnied in an agreeable manner. "Missouri Jim it is! Wee-hah!"

CHAPTER 3

ort Sanders wasn't much to look at. Nestled in a bend of the Laramie River, its ramshackle collection of log-and-sod buildings surrounded a dusty parade ground. With no tall wall to protect it, the fort looked more like a small village than a proper army post.

Fort Sanders commanded a view of the surrounding countryside and the hayfields that fed the fort's horses and livestock. Next to the cookhouse was a scraggly garden.

Besides the shabby barracks and officer's headquarters, there was a quartermaster's army supply house, a rickety stable, a post office, and a low-roofed one-room jail known as the guardhouse. There was also a sutler's store, a privately owned trade establishment where men could buy luxury items the army didn't provide.

Jane followed a party of blue-coated soldiers leading a train of pack mules loaded down with firewood. From atop the guard tower, a man's gruff voice called to Jane, "Halt! Who goes there?"

Jane lowered her voice as much as she could. "I'm Missouri Jim—scout."

The guard spit a stream of brown tobacco juice onto the ground. He peered skeptically at Jane and stroked his bristly gray beard. He fingered the long barrel of his Springfield carbine. "Maybe you are and maybe you ain't."

"That's enough of that," shouted a brusque, commanding voice.

Jane turned around and saw a handsome sergeant in a neat uniform. A line of polished brass buttons ran down his dark blue coat. Big yellow chevrons adorned the coat's sleeves. A broad leather belt with a shiny brass buckle stamped "U.S." held up a polished holster. The sergeant's trousers were light blue with a wide yellow stripe down the sides.

Jane marveled at the sergeant's tall, shiny boots. Beside him she felt as shabby as a shedding coyote.

The sergeant's broad tan hat shaded his bright blue eyes. A red mustache curved smartly above his smiling mouth. A yellow kerchief was knotted around his neck. He extended a yellow-gloved hand to Jane.

She jumped off her horse to shake. "Missouri Jim," Jane said.

"Sergeant Frank Siechrist," the soldier said. "We're looking for a scout. I'll take you to see Captain Egan."

"That's right—" Jane began in her normal voice. Then she cleared her throat and repeated, "That's right kind of you."

The sergeant examined Jane's smooth face. "How old are you?"

"Twenty-one," Jane said in her roughest, gruffest voice. "I'm mighty thirsty," she added, hoping to explain her squeaky voice.

"You can stop at the well," Sergeant Siechrist said. He

pointed toward the fort's pump. "I'll see you at headquarters."

"Thank you kindly," Jane muttered as the sergeant walked away.

The water from the pump was warm and rusty, but Jane didn't mind. She'd had worse from creeks and water holes.

Nearby, the firewood detail unloaded wood amid dogs and squawking chickens. A few dirty children romped in the dust. Their mothers were the camp laundresses on Suds Row, the name given to the cluster of shacks, tents, and shanties owned by women who made their living cleaning uniforms. Every fort had a Suds Row, because men who would put up with a lot in the service of their country drew the line at washing shirts. Watching the hard-faced women work, Jane remembered her own mother's chapped, red hands.

An old woman dripping suds from both arms shouted at a scrawny trooper, "You know we get more wood than that, son!"

The trooper snapped back, "Don't tell me what to do, you old hag. You're lucky to get *that* much. I've been out sweating with an ax all morning."

"She's right, Tuttle," chimed in a lanky trooper with a thick southern drawl.

"Stow it, Slaughter. You got the same number of stripes as me," Private Tuttle yelled.

The other members of the fuel detail dropped their logs to move closer to the action. Whenever Tuttle and Slaughter got together, sparks would fly. Always one to enjoy a good fight, Jane strolled over and mingled with the troopers.

"Regulations say these ladies are entitled to fuel, food, and medical attention," Private Slaughter asserted. "And you don't talk to a lady like that."

"You sure know regulations—for a reb!" Tuttle taunted.

Even though the Civil War had been over for eight years, many Americans still carried the scars of that terrible conflict. Northerners who defended the Union were known as Yankees, while those who had fought in the Confederate army of the South were still called rebs.

Private Slaughter's long face burned a dull red. He was sick of that Yankee teasing him. He fixed his cold blue eyes on Tuttle's face and slowly rolled his uniform sleeves to his elbows.

There were a few former Confederate soldiers among the fort's company of fifty men. Most got along fine. But now and again on hot days, or when Private Tuttle was being particularly disagreeable, tempers would flare.

The troopers placed bets. Slaughter was big, but Tuttle fought dirty.

"Fighting's against regulations, reb!" Tuttle taunted Slaughter.

Slaughter merely emitted a bloodcurdling yell and charged, his fists pumping. Jane's own fists twitched. She was itching to join the fun. "Let 'er rip!" she whooped.

Most of the men rooted for Slaughter because, despite his history in the Confederate army, he was an honorable man. Tuttle, however, was enough to make any soldier ashamed he had ever worn the Union blue.

Tuttle threw a handful of dust into Private Slaughter's eyes. Slaughter blindly grabbed at Tuttle's uniform and swung a powerful punch that connected with a thud. Tuttle flew off the ground and landed in a tub of suds.

"I'll get you!" Tuttle swore.

"You'll get clean first!" a private on the sidelines chuckled.

Jane laughed and slapped a dusty thigh.

Suddenly all the soldiers snapped to attention. Sergeant Siechrist barked, "Are you men fighting again? Who started it this time?"

Siechrist listened patiently to both sides of the story, then sentenced both privates to the punishment for insubordination. For the rest of the day, Tuttle and Slaughter had to march around the parade ground, each carrying a thirty-pound log.

Siechrist fixed a hard gaze on Jane. "I thought I told you to report to headquarters, carrot top."

Jane blushed. "I was just...headin' there when..." But Siechrist had already walked away. Jane hurried across the dusty parade ground to the low whitewashed headquarters. Corporal Racine, a mild-mannered orderly in a starched uniform, greeted Jane at the door and led her to Captain Egan's office. Egan was a barrel-chested old veteran with gray streaks in his dark hair and a weary cast to his stern features. Captain's bars gleamed on his shoulders, and a double row of brass buttons adorned his blue coat.

"What do you want?" Egan's black eyes looked Jane up and down.

"Missouri Jim's the name, scoutin's the game," Jane growled.

Egan sneered. "You? You don't even shave yet."

"I didn't know that shaving was part of the job," Jane said.

Egan smiled faintly. "Don't you have any manners?" he asked, looking at Jane's hat.

Jane whipped off her slouched hat. Her long red hair tumbled to her shoulders.

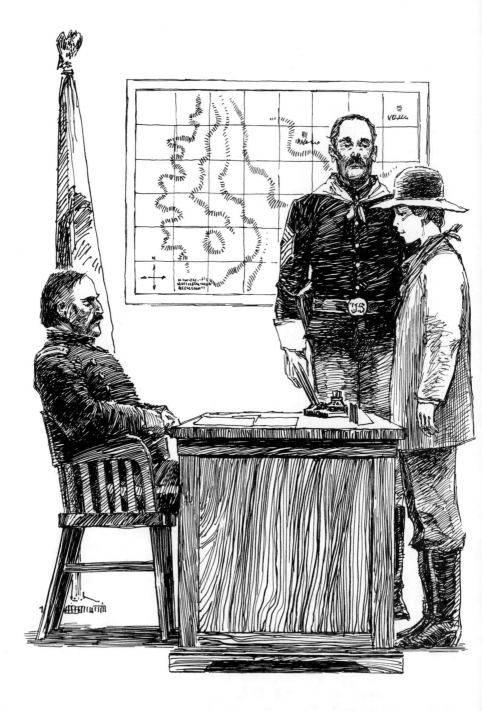

"Another Bill Cody, I see," the captain observed.

"Cody?" Jane replied. "Not only did he copy my hairstyle, but he learned all his scoutin' from me! 'Course he did teach me Indian sign language." Captain Egan looked skeptical.

"Actually, I learned sign from an old mountain man who was a personal friend of Buffalo Bill's," Jane confessed.

She went on to tell the captain of her experiences as a bullwhacker, pony express rider, stagecoach driver, and railroad track layer. If she stretched the truth a little, well, any halfway-decent scout was expected to tell tales. "Why, I know this country like the back of my hand. And I've wiggled out of more tight spots than a freckled rattlesnake in a speckled henhouse."

Egan filled a pipe and lit it. "Are you any good with that gun?"

"They don't call me Deadeye for nothin'!" Jane bragged.

Egan watched a few puffs of smoke drift lazily to the rough-timbered ceiling. "I thought your name was Missouri."

"Well, yes, sir, Captain, sir," Jane agreed. "It's Missouri Deadeye Jim."

"Any other names I should know about?" Egan asked.

Jane shook her head. Egan studied the ceiling. "We are shorthanded," he said at last. "Since the war ended, there aren't enough men in uniform. Our last scout was a Crow, and he got his hair lifted when he tangled with a party of Sioux with a personal grudge."

"Well, I don't know any Sioux personally, so I guess I'll be all right," Jane said with more confidence than she felt.

Captain Egan smiled. "The army's not here to fight the tribes anymore. President Grant has charged us with a mission to protect the red men's sacred lands up in the Black Hills. Conquest by kindness, he calls it. You've probably heard the rumors of gold in Dakota Territory."

Jane nodded. "Not much interest in it myself." Mining was backbreaking work. Jane had seen too many men die from the gold fever that made them work past their strength for an empty pan. Some had even killed their own brothers out of madness for the yellow rock.

"Well, you're alone in that," Egan said bitterly. "Times are hard, and there are plenty of fools out there who want to strike it rich. We've got our hands full trying to keep them from violating the Treaty of Fort Laramie. The Sioux don't take kindly to intruders. We're trying to keep the bloodshed to a minimum."

Jane nodded thoughtfully.

Egan sighed heavily, then continued. "Red Cloud is abiding by the treaties and is living on a reservation. But a lot of the young warriors can't stand reservation life. We know that there are crooked men working for the Indian agencies who take the rations and money that should be used to aid the tribes. That's enough to make anybody want to fight. Some braves just don't trust the government at all, and I can't say that I blame them."

"They're between a rock and a hard place," Jane agreed.

Egan nodded and puffed his pipe. "Sitting Bull and Spotted Tail, two powerful chiefs, occupy the north, up around the Bighorn. General Hancock and Colonel Custer want to wipe out *all* the tribes. Right now most of our troops are with General Crook chasing Cochise and his Apaches all over Arizona. I wish they'd just settle on the reservations. Chasing after wayward prospectors and ornery 'hostiles' is not the work of a real soldier," Egan added with a disdainful sniff. "But we follow orders as best we can. Fort Laramie has only a skeleton force. We're spread thin over a vast territory and outnumbered. I won't lie to you. Scouting is a dangerous job."

"Does that mean I'm hired?" Jane asked eagerly, trying to keep her voice from squeaking.

"Twenty dollars a month, and that's seven more than my troopers get. But you'll be the first into the fray," Egan replied.

Jane grinned.

"You seem like an able enough young man. Try to keep your head on your shoulders and your scalp on your head!" Egan urged. "The men are at chow. Grab yourself some beans. You can bunk in the barracks if you don't mind the bugs. Lord knows we've got plenty of empty bunks."

Jane grinned again, her heart thumping with excitement. Captain Egan saluted her briskly. Jane fumbled for a moment, not knowing which hand to raise in countersalute. She could hardly believe she had just been hired as an army scout!

"Dismissed," Captain Egan barked.

Jane hurried from his office, a blush burning her ears.

Soon she was looking around the cramped, stuffy barracks. Jane was none too picky about her surroundings, but this stifling, bug-ridden, rat-infested pit full of unwashed soldiers made a pigsty seem homey.

One bunk was occupied by a listless private with a greenish complexion. Jane knew scurvy when she saw it. The food here must be pretty bad, she thought. Jane determined that somehow she would eat vegetables.

"Don't bother looking for a bunk by a window," advised the sick soldier. "All the old-timers grab those in summer, just like they take the ones by the stove in the winter."

"What about that room?" Jane asked hopefully. She pointed to a door at the far end of the room.

"That's Sergeant Siechrist's quarters, boy. You can't sleep there till you earn your stripes," the soldier replied through cracked lips.

Jane decided she'd rather sleep outside. Besides the unsanitary conditions, there was no privacy. How could she keep her true identity secret in such close quarters?

That night, after the bugler played taps, Jane spread out her bedroll on the dusty parade ground. She stretched out and looked up at the stars. She could hear troopers singing in the barracks, where a lively card game was in progress.

"Psst, sonny," an old woman's husky voice called from a tent near the washtubs. "Sonny!"

At first, Jane didn't realize that the woman was talking to her.

"It's me, Kate," the old washerwoman said as she walked closer to Jane. "What're you doin' out here? Won't they let you sleep in the barracks?"

"It seems healthier out here, ma'am," Jane explained.

Kate smiled. "I wouldn't let my dog sleep in those barracks, but it's gonna get mighty cold out here. You can come stay in my tent. A nice young man like you shouldn't have to sleep outside without a fire."

Jane could see no graceful way to refuse the old woman's invitation, and already it was getting colder. So she slipped inside the cozy canvas tent.

"Make yourself at home," Kate urged. The old woman bumped into a crude table. "Land o' Goshen! I can't see a thing since I broke my specs. And the trader won't be around again till spring."

Jane was relieved. The old lady wouldn't be so quick to see anything unusual about the "young man." The two chatted for a while, Kate mainly talking about her husband, a sergeant killed back in 1867 while riding with Colonel Custer.

Jane fell asleep thinking of her family. Although she had had five younger siblings—two brothers and three sisters— only a brother, Elijah, and a sister, Lena, were still alive. The rest had fallen victim to disease and harsh winters. After the death of Jane's parents, a kindly couple had taken in the two younger children, but because nobody wanted a wild teenager, Jane had been forced to go her own way. She hadn't seen Lena or Elijah since then, but Jane hoped that wherever they were, they were happy.

CHAPTER 4

The bugle sounded reveille at 5:30 A.M. Jane didn't see any point in waking up before the sun rose, but there was no sleeping with the noise of fifty men getting chow and preparing for their drills at 6:15.

Jane watched the soldiers march in formation and lead their highly trained horses through complicated drills. After an hour, the men fell out for fatigue duty, which Jane learned meant garbage detail, stable cleaning, gardening, and fetching wood and water.

At the 7:15 bugle call, the men turned out before the barracks to have their spanking-clean uniforms inspected by their sergeant. Then they marched to the parade ground for an inspection by the captain.

Jane thought it was strange that Captain Egan never spoke directly to the men but gave his orders first to Sergeant Siechrist, who would then shout commands to the troopers.

The sergeant announced assignments to posts, and then the men performed the manual of arms, drilling with their rifles. The password of the day was issued, and guards were posted.

Tuttle griped when Corporal Racine was named orderly

of the day again. "Just because he sits up half the night blacking his shoes and polishing buttons, he gets away without duty."

"Maybe if you weren't such a wrinkled mess of sorry Yankee swill, you'd get to hang about headquarters and the kitchen," Slaughter countered.

O'Hara stepped between the angry privates. "Now, don't start it again, boys."

Over the next few weeks, Jane grew more comfortable being Missouri Jim. The men joshed about her squeaky voice and small hands, but they soon accepted her as one of the gang. Even Egan found the "boy's" high spirits and wild stories amusing. Missouri Jim stopped being a novelty and became part of daily life at Fort Sanders.

Jane, however, quickly grew bored watching the endless drilling and listening to the endless griping. She was glad when scouting duties—such as hunting for fresh meat and helping the wood detail find firewood—sent her out of the fort.

Still, the long afternoons at the fort were almost as bad as being back in Piedmont. Jane planned to use her scout pay to buy supplies for the day when she moved on. She had been on the trail most of her life and didn't intend to stop now. The way Jane figured things, there were always new places to go and new people to meet. The rigid routine of Fort Sanders was starting to pinch like a tight pair of boots.

Jane already knew everyone's story by heart. Racine used to be a clerk but got bored with his dull job. He thought the army would be more exciting.

Tuttle was a bookkeeper all the way from someplace

called the Bowery in New York City, which was some big town back east. Word had it that Tuttle had done something crooked, but men knew better than to ask too many questions. Half the men in the army weren't even signed up under their real names, for various reasons.

Slaughter was a Tennessee farm boy who had joined the army looking for adventure. After the war, he hadn't wanted to return to the drudgery of his daddy's farm, so he had reenlisted.

Chandler had been a dentist but found out that he didn't like the sight of blood. He bunked beside Old Crabtree.

Crabtree had signed up for seven hitches in a row— thirty-five years! He'd been at Fort Sanders so long, Jane doubted he could remember what decent food tasted like.

Ross was the soldier suffering from scurvy. He had been a drummer—a traveling salesman drumming up business for a line of ladies' corsets. He could talk a blue streak and sell shoes to a snake. But after the war, money got scarce, and even a crackerjack salesman like Ross couldn't earn a living. So he'd signed up as a "temporary measure"—eight years ago.

Ross's bunkie O'Hara had come all the way from Ireland to work on the Union Pacific railroad. But it was finished by the time O'Hara reached Wyoming Territory, so he reasoned that joining the army was better than starving on the plains.

Most of the troopers were excellent riders. But because bullets were expensive, they didn't get any target practice. Jane was probably as good a shot as any man in the company.

The men whooped and hollered when payday finally came. Once every two months was a long time to wait for their money *and* a day off, and the troopers fidgeted on the line before the paymaster's desk.

Jane was looking forward to buying some bullets at the quartermaster's store. But when she saw the army's paper money, Jane shrieked, "What is this?"

"That's your pay," Paymaster Dibbs barked. He was a fat man with ink-stained fingers and a few strands of hair combed over his pink scalp.

"This ain't money," Jane complained. "Where's the gold? Where's the silver? Where's the coin?"

"If you want civilian money, you ride over to Laramie and exchange this," Dibbs advised curtly. "Step aside."

Sergeant Siechrist laughed. "I wouldn't recommend that. You can lose up to forty percent when you exchange."

Old Crabtree laughed. "Nobody gets rich in this man's army."

That was true. In short order, most of the men spent their earnings at the sutler's store. Jane bought twelve bullets and stowed the precious pellets in her saddlebags with a small roll of money and some canned goods. She didn't bother with the overpriced chewing tobacco but stocked up on canned fruit and canned meat and beans. She got herself some soap, a comb, and a needle and thread to patch up her clothes. If things got too boring, Jane figured she would have enough provisions to get her to the next town.

Jane paid Kate for the use of her washtub and tent for a bath. The old woman was surprised at the scout's modesty but figured that Jim was just a decent young man with better manners than most of the other troopers.

Soldiers were supposed to bathe once a week, but there were no bathhouses at the fort, so they traded tobacco for the use of the Suds Row washtubs. Most men preferred tobacco to baths, which accounted for their rancid smell. The horses were cleaner than the men who rode them. Only Corporal Racine and Sergeant Siechrist seemed to have more than a passing acquaintance with soap and water.

For the rest of the afternoon, the men played horseshoes on the parade ground. Jane joined in but lost to Old Crabtree.

"Horseshoes isn't my game," she said. "Now, horse racing—that's another story."

Crabtree grinned. "Talkin's more like it. You're on, if you're man enough to race a cavalry rider."

Jane adjusted the bandanna covering her smooth neck. She swaggered a little before answering in her lowest voice. "Twice man enough, and Jim's four times the horse."

"We'll see about that—ten laps around the fort!" Old Crabtree challenged Jane. He spit a fine stream of brown tobacco juice at her feet.

"Prepare to lose!" Jane replied.

"We'll just see, sonny." The old man hoisted himself into the saddle of a spirited bay.

Four other soldiers mounted their horses and lined up at the gate. They couldn't waste a bullet on a starting shot, so the bugler played to start the race.

Jim took off like a jackrabbit, and Jane leaned low over his neck while his hooves pounded and raised the dust all around her. Crabtree started off right beside her, but Jim inched ahead, and for the last two laps, there was no question who would win.

The rest of the garrison cheered and threw their hats in the air when the scout reached the gate. With great ceremony, Sergeant Siechrist awarded Jane the prize—a can of peaches.

When Jane walked Jim back to the stable, Siechrist

followed. He hung around the stall while Jane brushed Jim's sweaty flanks.

"That was right exciting!" Jane said, struggling to keep her voice low.

"Getting bored, eh?" Siechrist asked. "That's the army. Sit around and wait, and then suddenly things are hopping."

"I'm not much good at waiting," Jane admitted. She filled a feed bag with oats and hung it over Jim's muzzle.

"If you think this is boring, you should hear Egan when he's feeling talkative. Sometimes he orders me into his quarters just to repeat his exploits in the glorious War Between the States. To hear him tell it," Siechrist said with a twinkle in his blue eyes, "Egan was the brains behind Sheridan, Sherman, and Ulysses S. Grant himself."

Jane laughed. "Why isn't he president?"

"He asks himself the same question," Frank said, and they laughed.

Realizing her laughter had sounded a bit too high, Jane cleared her throat. "Must be the dust," she grumbled. Then she went back to brushing Jim.

Siechrist stared at Jane's hands while she worked. "You've got mighty small hands," he said.

"All the men in my family have small hands," she said gruffly. "Never stopped us from getting our work done."

The sergeant shrugged amiably. His blue eyes peered into Jane's. She looked down at the brush in her hand and swallowed hard. Jane had seen the same curious look on Siechrist's face before. She wondered if he suspected her disguise. But what could she do?

Siechrist pulled a twist of chewing tobacco out of his

jacket pocket. He tucked a plug in his mouth. "Don't like to chew in front of the men," he explained. "The captain thinks it looks undignified. But since you're just a scout, would you care for a chaw?"

Siechrist held the dense block of brown leaves out to Jane.

Jane hesitated, then flaked off a small wad. "Uh...thanks, don't mind if I do." She couldn't turn down Frank's offer: She had to seem like just one of the guys, so Jane tucked the plug between her cheek and her gums, just as she'd seen the soldiers do. Suddenly her mouth filled with the most hideous bitter, salty taste. She wanted to gag but thought she might choke first.

"Good tobacco, don't you think?" Siechrist asked politely.

Jane struggled to smile around a mouthful of soggy leaves. She saw a glimmer of amusement in Siechrist's eyes.

"You've never chewed before, have you, sonny?" the sergeant asked.

"Sure I have," Jane said, brown juice dribbling down her chin.

The sergeant gave her a skeptical look and spit contentedly onto the straw. "Nothing like a chaw to make a man relax," Frank said. "You'll get used to it. The army'll make a man of you."

Jane nodded vigorously. Siechrist turned to leave. With great relief, Jane waved good-bye, and as soon as the sergeant had left the barn, she spit out the nasty mess. Jane rinsed her mouth with Jim's bucket of water to flush out the foul flavor.

Chewing tobacco wasn't the only bad taste at the fort: there was breakfast, lunch, and dinner. Jane could hardly believe how bad the monotonous meals tasted.

Each day was the same: Beef hash, dry sliced bread, and coffee for breakfast. Sliced beef, dry bread, and coffee for lunch. And supper was dry bread and coffee.

"Feed up to the limit while you can. You'll need a hump like a camel in the field," advised Old Crabtree, who shoveled down chow as if he had no taste buds.

The awful quality of the food was partly because all the supplies were hauled long distances by slow wagons. If the bacon was already half-spoiled, it now had a chance to truly ripen, and the weevils got a good jump on the flour. Mice nested deep in supply barrels—unless they got chased out by rats.

But the main problem was the army practice of having each trooper take a turn as cook. Siechrist explained that the goal was to teach the men to be self-reliant in the field. Jane didn't think that was a good enough reason to accept such poor food. As a scout, she was exempt from this duty, but she had to suffer its consequences.

Old Crabtree grumbled, "Why, this chow's killed more troopers than all the arrows in the West!"

Jane chuckled. "Doesn't seem to stop you from cleaning your plate."

Crabtree nodded toward Jane. "I'll finish that beef, if you aren't."

Jane happily handed the old trooper her plate. "I guess I haven't been at the fort long enough to lose my taste buds."

Crabtree smiled around a full mouth. Then he said, "Just give it time, sonny."

*   *   *

Jane could soon tell whose cooking she was eating. Corporal Racine could fix a tolerable mess of beans, with just a touch of molasses. But Private Tuttle was forever letting the food burn while he lost himself in dime novels.

One afternoon, Jane stepped into the mess hall and recognized the wretched smell of scorched beans. She knew Tuttle the Terrible had struck again.

Jane slammed down her tin plate after one bite and spit out the blackened beans. "Enough is enough. Let me at that kitchen!"

Jane picked up Tuttle by the scruff of his neck, and his well-thumbed *Deadeye Dick* magazine dropped to the dirt floor. Jane had never been fond of cooking, although she had worked in a restaurant. "Get out of here while I cook some real food," Jane growled. Tuttle put up his fists, ready to fight. But Jane had already turned her back on him to face the stove.

There wasn't much to work with. The army's idea of food consisted of beans, hardtack biscuits, bacon, flour, and coffee. Sometimes there was low-grade range beef, and occasionally a hunting party brought in a gamey pronghorn antelope or a brace of jackrabbits. For seasoning, there was salt, brown sugar, vinegar, and molasses.

Jane did the best she could, but her beans with chipped beef did not meet with much enthusiasm among the men. Jane was no Corporal Racine.

Tuttle balked at the sticky beans. "This is the worst food I've ever tasted."

Tired and cross from the hot iron stove, Jane leveled her Colt at Tuttle's scraggly head. "Eat beans or eat lead, pardner."

The mess hall echoed with the clattering din of forks on

tin plates. Everyone stared at Jane and Tuttle, waiting to see what would happen next.

Sergeant Siechrist glared at Jane. "Okay, scout. Hand over the iron." He held out his large hand for Jane's pistol.

Jane shuffled her feet. "Aw, shucks, Frank. It ain't even loaded."

Sergeant Siechrist tried to hide his grin. "Let's keep it that way," he said.

CHAPTER 5

Who goes there?" Private Slaughter called from the guard tower.

"Jedediah Blackburn," replied the worn, dusty driver slouched in a wagon seat. His pinch-faced wife and scrawny children huddled behind him in the straw bed of the wagon. "You gotta help us. They're going to kill us all!"

Slaughter nodded, and the wagon rattled onto the parade ground. The private yelled for Corporal Racine, who fetched Sergeant Siechrist.

"Who is gonna kill us all?" the sergeant asked calmly.

Jane sidled up to see what all the excitement was about. The farmer's wife peered suspiciously at the scout from beneath her stiff bonnet.

Jane had seen an expression like hers before. Frontier farmers spent months in complete isolation, and when they finally did poke their faces into a town, they were as wary of people as they were of wild dogs.

The Blackburn children stared at everything with big solemn eyes and stared all the harder when Jane smiled at them.

Mr. Blackburn went on, breathlessly. "There's a bunch of them Indians snooping around our land. We saw them riding after a couple of fellers, whooping and hollering to beat all!"

"Get the captain," Siechrist told Racine, who hurried to headquarters. The sergeant turned back to the farmer. "Who were these 'fellers'—neighbors of yours?"

Blackburn shook his head. "I never seen 'em before they rode through a couple of weeks ago. Said they were headin' north. Yesterday, I was out pulling weeds, and they come flying across my cornfield with hundreds of them feathered heathens on their heels."

"Hundreds? Are you sure?" Siechrist asked.

Mr. Blackburn swallowed hard. "Well, maybe not. But it sure seemed like a whole lot of 'em, with the hollering and all."

The sergeant nodded. He had heard reports from terrified settlers before. Ten braves seemed like a hundred to a man afraid his family might be captured and his farm burned.

Sometimes a lone tribesman hunting deer was enough to send settlers racing to the fort for protection. But there were also instances when, despite signs of trouble, others stubbornly stayed on their farms only to die on the fields they had plowed.

Siechrist was sure the captain would at least want to investigate Blackburn's story, as it was the fort's mission to keep track of any Indians and, if possible, to preserve peace in the territory.

Captain Egan listened thoughtfully as the farmer repeated his tale. "Why didn't you go to Fort Laramie?" he asked.

"Why, there's Indians camped all around there," Blackburn explained.

"It's a trading post," Sergeant Siechrist said. "Those are peaceful tribes."

"They're all dangerous, if you ask me," the farmer said. He spit on the ground.

"No one asked you," Egan said. "Sergeant, see about quarters for these people." Excitement glimmered in his dark eyes. The old battle fever stirred in the captain's blood. "Have the troops ready to mount up in half an hour."

Siechrist saluted smartly and hurried off. Egan swung around to Jane. "Well, scout, let's see how good you are."

"Let 'er rip!" Jane cheered and ran for the stables to saddle Jim.

For the next half hour the fort was the busiest place Jane had ever seen. Corporal Racine was placed in charge of the fort while Sergeant Siechrist and Captain Egan prepared to lead about half the men into the field.

Weapons were issued to the troops, and the hot air soon became thick with the mixed smells of gun oil and saddle soap used on the leather shoulder straps. Two pack mules were outfitted with medical supplies and additional ammunition.

Jane liked to travel light and was alarmed to see how much the cavalry carried. Each horse was loaded with 150 rounds of ammunition, half a pup tent, a blanket, a rubber ground sheet, and extra uniforms. Saddlebags bulged with grain for the horses and food for the troopers for seven days.

"This won't last long if them Indians lead us on a merry chase," Crabtree griped. He tossed a bit of beef jerky to one of the camp dogs. "You come along with us, Blue." Crabtree winked at Jane. "Dog's good meat if you get hungry enough, sonny."

Jane wasn't sure if the old veteran was joking. She'd known miners desperate enough to eat moccasin thongs or black cricket stew.

Jane had never been hungry enough to cook crickets, and she hoped she never would be. "Don't worry, Crabtree. I'll find us grub along the trail."

"You'd better find those Indians, too!" Tuttle said. He hefted his Springfield. "It's about time we used these rifles for something besides drills."

In addition to a rifle, each trooper wore a Colt revolver on his hip. Captain Egan also carried a curved saber even though soldiers usually left them behind. Plains warriors rarely got close enough for a sword to be effective. Jane supposed the captain was thinking of his glory days battling the Confederates.

The bugler sounded boots and saddles, and the mounted troopers assembled behind Siechrist and Egan. O'Hara proudly carried the company colors on a long lance. The supply mules brought up the rear.

Jane took her place at the head of the column, beside Egan. She felt like she had swallowed a pitcher full of butterflies.

"Wee-hah!" Jane hollered as the column rode four abreast out the gate.

Twenty-seven men and their horses sure made a lot of noise! Hooves thudded on the dry ground, and rattling cups and skillets swung from creaking saddles and harnesses. The horses snorted and whinnied, and the stubborn mules brayed.

Soldiers complained or sang to fill the sudden emptiness of the lonely windswept plain. They had left their safe fort far behind and were on their own.

After her first rush of excitement, Jane quickly settled down. She knew they wouldn't find the Indians right away. They might be on the trail for days or weeks.

That day, they stopped early and set up camp. Normally scouts rode ahead of the troop to be on the lookout for danger or to follow a trail. But in this case, Jane rode with the men. She wouldn't start tracking the warriors until they had all reached Blackburn's farm.

Jane had just gotten used to the early hours at the fort, but on the trail the troops rose even earlier. First call sounded at 4:45. The men hardly had time to roll out of their blankets before the bugler sounded reveille and stable call. Everybody would saddle and hitch and then eat breakfast.

Jane had barely choked down her food when it was time to strike camp. As the last tent was packed, the bugler blew boots and saddles, and they were off.

The troop rode for four hours, then rested the animals for two hours; the cavalry would be nothing without healthy horses.

The men rode a few more hours, then set up camp. The horses and mules were arranged in a line and fed and watered. Guards were posted to look out for Indians or wild animals. Details were sent out for water and buffalo chips for fires. The rest of the troopers assembled the pup tents, each bunkie contributing half of the canvas and poles.

Jane cooked a mess of beans over a fire she shared with Crabtree and Chandler. She greedily wolfed down her share of the sticky beans.

"There's nothing like hunger to make any slop taste good," Old Crabtree observed. He mopped his gooey plate with a biscuit. "We'll be seeing some action tomorrow," he declared.

"What makes you say that?" Jane asked.

Crabtree tapped his left thigh. "Old arrow wound. Starts hurting every time we're near Indians. You mark my words, sonny, and clean your pistol!"

Sergeant Siechrist strolled up to the fire carrying a battered skillet. He looked from Jane to her plate, which was scraped clean. "Looks like you've got room for dessert. When I was a boy I was always hungry, too."

Jane sniffed the sweet aroma and leaned closer to peer inside the skillet. "What is it?"

"Hardtack fried in bacon grease and sprinkled with brown sugar," Siechrist explained as he broke off a piece for Jane.

"I'm not a boy," she protested around a full mouth.

Siechrist chuckled. "Well, you sure eat like one!"

The next day, the troop reached the Blackburns' sod hut on a creek near the North Platte River. Willow trees and cottonwoods dotted the scraggly brush on the creek's banks.

Jane scanned the fields for a sign—any mark that would point out a trail. She spotted the wobbly tracks of Blackburn's wagon and the prints of the farmer's boots in the corn patch.

Horseshoe prints revealed to Jane where the settlers had passed. A line of crushed cornstalks showed where the warriors had pursued them. The settlers' prints were trampled by the large, unshod hoofprints of the warriors' ponies.

The Cheyennes rode small mountain ponies. Members of the Blackfoot tribe rode ponies that were only slightly bigger. Jane knew that the Lakota Sioux rode the largest horses of all the tribes in the territory.

"They're Sioux," Jane told Egan. "Not more than ten braves. Looks like they headed off these fellers and circled back north."

The captain frowned. "They're headed for the safety of the Black Hills. There might be a larger force elsewhere, and these were just an advance party of scouts."

Jane shrugged. "Reckon the only way we'll find out for sure is by following that trail." And follow the trail they did—northeast for three days straight across the drought-stricken landscape toward the Black Hills, looming in the distance.

Jane rode ahead of the main troop, looking for a sign. She could feel the blazing sun beating down on her, and even though she had her neckerchief tied across her nose and mouth, she still tasted dust.

Jane dismounted when she came upon hoofprints and horse dung. She saw that shod hoofprints had crushed the buffalo grass and left behind flecks of sand. Jane concluded that these horses had passed in the morning, when there was still dew, because sand from their hooves would stick to grass only when it was wet.

There were hoofprints from unshod ponies as well. These had also flattened the grass, but there were no traces of sand; their trail had been made after the sun had dried the dew. Thus, the Sioux ponies were hours behind the settlers' horses.

Judging by the long distance between each animal's hoofprints, Jane knew that the settlers' horses were galloping past exhaustion. The overlapping hoofprints of the Sioux ponies meant that they were trotting at a steady but comfortable pace. The dung was dried enough to indicate that the cavalry was days behind.

Private Slaughter galloped up to Jane. "The captain says find water."

Jane frowned. "We ought to stay on this trail before it gets any older."

Slaughter shrugged. "Orders." He turned his horse and rode back to the main column. Jane followed him.

"Captain, sir, I still find no sign of any more than those ten braves," Jane reported. "I reckon that farmer was just wild with fear."

Egan nodded sourly. He was disappointed to be chasing a few braves on the word of some hysterical farmer. They had been on the march for nearly a week, and supplies were running low.

"This looks like a wild goose chase," Egan told Jane. "Let's call it good exercise for the men and get back to the fort. But first, find some water, scout."

Jane was disappointed. She'd hoped to see some real army action.

Judging by the curves of the hills and valleys, by the vegetation, and finally by the smell of the tepid breeze, Jane led the troop to a bubbling creek sunk between rocky banks. A loaded pack mule grazed nearby.

"Now who would leave a perfectly good mule?" Jane wondered. She and Egan examined the mule's burden: pickaxes, gold pans, and other prospecting gear.

Jane knew from her father's gold-panning days that prospecting gear was expensive. Most prospectors would rather die than abandon their tools. "Looks like those fellers chased across Blackburn's farm got cured of their gold fever in a hurry," she observed.

Captain Egan nodded. "Prospectors wouldn't set their mule free unless they were desperate. Well, the poor devils are probably dead by now," he concluded. "And if those Sioux have made it back to Dakota Territory, we can't touch them even if we find them. We'll head back to the fort after we rest the horses."

While Jane and Egan talked, the soldiers wasted no time stripping off their sweaty uniforms to swim in the cool creek. Siechrist and a couple of other men stood guard, but they weren't expecting trouble. The warriors they were pursuing were probably miles away by now.

"What're you waiting for?" Old Crabtree called to Jane from the water.

"Oh, I can't swim," Jane fibbed. She was dying for a dip but didn't dare take off her bulky buckskins.

Captain Egan was surprised. "A strapping young lad like you?"

"You sure you ain't just scared?" Tuttle teased.

"I'm not scared of anything!" Jane declared. Suddenly she found herself surrounded by joking soldiers who pulled off her gun belt and threw her into the water.

"Wee-hah, that feels good!" Jane shouted. But no one else shouted. They stared open-mouthed at Jane. The scout's wet buckskins clung in such a way that even the most near-sighted trooper knew at a glance that Missouri Jim was not a lad but a lass.

"Well, what's the difference?" Jane shouted crossly. "I found the trail, didn't I, and this here water?" Jane looked to Old Crabtree. "And I whupped you in that horse race fair and square!"

Egan blustered, "This is highly irregular. Regulations are clear. You will have to find other employment as soon as we return to the fort."

"Not again!" Jane bellowed.

Siechrist chuckled. "Guess you aren't a boy, after all. But if you're not Missouri Jim, who are you?"

Jane extended a wet hand to the sergeant. "Martha Jane Cannary. Pleased to make your acquaintance."

CHAPTER 6

Jane looked around at the stunned faces of the troop. The mixture of shock and alarm seemed way out of proportion to the revelation of her identity. Then she followed Chandler's gaze to the opposite bank of the creek.

A small band of Lakota braves stared back at the troopers. Their decorated ponies pawed the ground and snorted.

A shiver of fear tingled up Jane's spine. Though she'd spent days looking for the Sioux, it was a shock to have them suddenly appear. Like the Cheyenne she'd seen on her way out of Piedmont, these braves had shown up quickly and quietly, like a menacing mirage.

A hasty movement at Jane's left finally made her look away. Tuttle sloshed to shore and snatched up his revolver. Before anyone else could react, he fired.

The sound of the shot boomed through the small valley. Jane saw one of the braves lifted off his pony by the bullet's impact. He clutched his chest and started to fall off his unsaddled mount. But he was quickly caught by one of his companions.

Anger flashed through Jane to the roots of her red hair. That darn fool Tuttle had done it. If the braves hadn't come for a fight, they were sure to want one now.

The Lakota braves reared on their ponies and shook their bows over their heads in a gesture meant to frighten the enemy. A ferocious war cry split the air. Jane's knees turned to jelly. She had heard that the war cry of a Plains brave had won more battles than had arrows, and now she knew why. Although the troopers outnumbered the braves by about five to one, the Sioux seemed not the least bit afraid.

"I knew my drumstick was hurtin'," Crabtree shouted. He splashed for the bank in his soggy underwear. The other soldiers cussed and floundered for the shore.

Jane scrambled out of the water to scoop up her gun belt. She wedged herself behind fallen boulders and loaded her pistol with shaking hands.

"If I ever get out of this, I'll become a schoolmarm," Jane resolved. She peeked out from behind the rock to fire a few shots in the general direction of the attacking braves.

Now Jane knew why Egan missed the neat lines of uni-formed men who had fought in the Civil War. This was chaos!

Painted ponies splashed across the creek. Their riders were a blur of feathers and fluttering fringe.

The troopers still stuck in the creek flapped and dripped up the slippery bank.

Jane covered her ears as shots boomed all around her. Arrows zinged through the air and peppered the ground. Only one brave carried a rifle, which he swung like a club.

"Circle and shield!" Captain Egan bellowed, and Siechrist echoed the order.

The soldiers yanked short carbine rifles from the leather scabbards on their saddles.

They forced their horses to lie down, then flattened themselves behind these living shields to aim their single-shot Springfields.

"Fire at will, boys! Give them a lead bath!" Egan screamed.

Jane peeked above her boulder long enough to spot the Lakota leader. He waved a long iron-tipped lance in his powerful fist. Many feathers, signifying past victories, decorated his glossy black braids.

"That's the chief," Egan yelled. "Shoot him and the others will back off."

Jane had a clear shot at the leader. She leveled her Colt at his broad, muscular chest. But she couldn't pull the trigger. She had no argument with this man.

The leader's horse rode straight into the muzzles of the cavalry carbines, through a hail of bullets whizzing past his flying braids. Jane shuddered, expecting at any moment to see the magnificent warrior tumble from his pony. But he rode on fearlessly, untouched by the cavalry bullets.

He's lucky these men never have target practice, Jane thought. The suddenness of the attack, which had literally caught the troop with its pants down, wasn't helping anyone's aim, either.

Only Old Crabtree seemed calm and focused despite the noise and confusion. Jane watched him take careful aim and squeeze off a shot that dropped a Sioux off his pony. The fallen brave was quickly scooped up by his comrades.

Jane saw the Lakota leader's pony leap over the circle of cavalry horses.

What in the name of heaven is he doing? she wondered.

The young warrior leaned low over the pony's neck to tap Egan on the shoulder with his decorated stick. Jane could hardly believe her eyes. The leader was counting coup! In wars between Plains tribes, the bravest warriors scored points of honor by showing that they *could* have killed their enemy— by tapping him with a special coup stick.

Captain Egan turned white with shock and fear. Siechrist whirled around to aim at the warrior. But the brave was a blur of motion as his pony vaulted the ring of horses.

Before Siechrist could fire, an arrow pierced his right shoulder. The sergeant's pistol fell to the dust as he sank to his knees.

Counting coup had the same effect on the troop that it would have on another tribe. The Sioux leader had shown his superiority to Captain Egan, and Jane realized with a rush of terror that the troop might not win this battle. So she was not surprised when Tuttle dropped his rifle and ran.

"Shoot that deserter!" Egan commanded in a shaky voice.

Crabtree popped a few bullets at Tuttle's feet, but the little man just ran faster. Jane ducked her head back down and fumbled to reload her pistol.

Arrows rained down on the soldiers. Several troopers screamed in pain. Crabtree made his way over to the sergeant. The head of the warrior's arrow was still embedded in Siechrist's shoulder. Crabtree grabbed ahold of the arrow's shaft and tried to pull it out.

Jane heard Siechrist's agonized gasp. She wanted to help him, but she was separated from the rest of the troop. She wouldn't be able to rejoin them until the battle was over—one way or another.

Jane slapped her empty pockets, looking for bullets. She drew her bowie knife but hoped she wouldn't have to use it.

The warriors charged again. They rode without saddles, moving as one with their galloping mounts.

Battle strategies and military history, past glories and the terrifying face of the Lakota leader all flashed through Captain Egan's mind. Though he was ashamed to even be thinking it, retreat seemed the only logical course. Properly trained soldiers might fend off such an attack, but these unclad amateurs were so unnerved by the Sioux, they could barely reload their weapons.

"Remount into battle formation!" Egan screeched, waving his saber wildly. He planned a leapfrog withdrawal, which meant the men would cover each other in alternating rows while they backed up the hill.

"Remount!" Egan shouted again. But no one was listening.

Egan felt a sudden stab of hot pain. He looked down to see the long, feathered shaft of a Lakota arrow poking out of a neat, red hole in his thigh.

Egan's leg seemed very far away from him as his eyes clouded with shock from his wound. The war cries and gunshots faded into a quiet, distant buzzing while Egan calmly studied his thigh as if it belonged to someone else.

The arrow was feathered almost halfway up the slender shaft and decorated with painted rings. Suddenly Egan's leg collapsed underneath him, but before he hit the ground, strong hands seized him under both armpits, and he felt himself being lifted between two braves.

Crabtree shot another brave as the band of Sioux galloped off into the distance. Hit in the shoulder, the Lakota reeled, but he clutched his pony's mane and rode on.

Jane popped out of her hiding place to join the troopers. "We've gotta save the captain!" she hollered. "Who's with me?"

The men milled around, pulling on pants and jackets and boots. They wrapped bandages around each other's wounds.

Siechrist croaked orders to the shaken and discouraged soldiers.

"Shouldn't we wait for reinforcements?" Private Slaughter asked.

"Who sent for 'em?" Jane asked. "Is that where Tuttle was goin'?"

Crabtree chuckled.

"I'll lead the rescue," Siechrist said. He put one foot in his stirrup. Then his eyes rolled up, and he flopped into the dust like a rag doll.

Jane grabbed Slaughter's sleeve. "See to his bleeding and make sure he gets back to the fort in one piece." Jane wished she could be in two places at once—nursing Siechrist and rescuing Captain Egan.

"You goin' to rescue the captain all by yourself?" Old Crabtree asked.

"If I can," Jane declared defiantly. "At least I can see where they've taken him and report back his position."

Crabtree nodded. "Might be a good idea. But I'd wait for orders before goin' ahead and doing it."

"Then at least loan me some bullets," Jane said impatiently. "Every moment's delay could mean the captain's life."

Crabtree filled her hands with lead pellets. "If I were twenty years younger, I'd go with you. Good luck, sonny! I mean, missy."

Siechrist lifted his head from the dirt. "Hold on there, Miss Cannary. The captain said you're not scoutin' for us. You stay here."

"Well, I've never been much for doing what I was told. And I don't aim to start by letting a good man die," Jane declared. She swung up into Jim's saddle and rode off after the thundering Sioux ponies.

CHAPTER 7

Jane tracked the warriors to their campsite in a little wooded valley. She knew the Sioux must have posted guards, so she circled around to the back of a gully, a trench worn in the soil by heavy rains.

She climbed off Jim, tied his bridle to a pine tree, and loaded her Colt, wincing at the sound of each soft clank of metal.

Creeping through the fragrant pines and underbrush, Jane strained to be quiet, but the dry, rustling grass sounded as loud as thunder to her nervous ears.

The blazing sun flashed between the trees. Jane realized that it wouldn't set for hours. If she was to try to rescue Egan, she'd have to wait for darkness.

Reminding herself to pause between steps and to breathe in quiet, measured breaths, Jane finally approached the campsite. She could hardly believe she'd gotten so far without the sharp-eared braves noticing. She peeked cautiously through the branches and saw Captain Egan tied up with leather thongs. Jane was relieved to see that his wound was freshly bandaged. The captain looked pale but alert.

The Lakotas' ponies were tethered off to one side, and among them were two exhausted saddled horses that Jane figured belonged to the prospectors. She thought they must be lying dead somewhere.

Most of the warriors were watching a small cave at the end of the valley. Two stood guard near its mouth. Jane wondered if they'd trapped a bear inside.

But when a shot echoed from the mouth of the cavern, she reckoned that the prospectors were holed up there. If the Sioux had had bullets of their own, she reasoned, they would have fired them during the battle.

A tall warrior strung his bow and shot an arrow into the cave. Jane heard someone cuss from inside the dark hole. But when no more shots or arrows were fired, she turned her attention back to Captain Egan.

The Lakota leader stood over the captain, trying to talk to him in sign language. Jane couldn't understand the signs from where she was crouching in the trees. All she could make out was Egan's puzzled face.

No wonder the army needs scouts, Jane thought crossly. The darn fools don't even know sign language!

Jane recognized the Lakota leader from the battle, but now she could see him more clearly. His dark, intelligent eyes were set close over a long, broad nose. Black spots adorned his broad chest, which was partly covered by a small bone breastplate with dangling feathers.

The leader wore a loincloth and wide, beaded deerskin leggings and moccasins. A claw necklace circled his throat, and a hunting knife hung at his hip.

Jane saw him point over and over to the cave. But Egan

just shook his head. Jane watched for a while and tried to put the facts together on her own. Clearly two prospectors had been trespassing on Sioux land in the Black Hills. The war party had chased them out of the hills and pursued them across the Blackburns' farm and finally to this cave. Since the Treaty of Fort Laramie stated that settlers had to be punished by United States authorities, the Sioux might have been deliberately chasing the prospectors to Fort Sanders. But Jane might never know the truth—Tuttle had confused everything by starting the fight.

Her eyes wandered to the cave. Were the prospectors really in there? Why didn't the Sioux just storm the cave? Were they waiting for the trapped prospectors to run out of bullets?

Finally, the leader gave up trying to communicate with Captain Egan. One of the braves asked the leader a question, and the man's answering shrug perfectly expressed his frustration.

Jane suddenly saw these tribesmen in a new light. They were just people who liked to hunt and fish, same as she did. All they wanted was to be left alone on their own land, to be free to live as they chose.

But how could the Sioux go on as they had for centuries when the settlers were slaughtering buffalo by the thousands? Game *and* land were getting awfully scarce. And between the Eulalia Beecrofts and greedy prospectors crowding the frontier, freedom was becoming more rare than gold.

Jane couldn't blame the Sioux or any other tribe for not wanting to be cooped up on the reservation, eating rotten beef and weevily grain. They'd been living on the Plains for generations, hunting buffalo and living as free as the breeze.

Jane watched the braves cooking supper. She saw the leader carry a wooden bowl over to Egan. This man, who had been so fierce in battle, was now being gentle and courteous. She saw him speak soothing words to his injured companions, and he encouraged the wounded men to eat and drink.

Jane was no longer so sure about her plan to go back to the fort to report Egan's position. Somehow, after watching the braves quietly prepare their supper, she didn't have the stomach to set them up for an ambush. There had to be another way to free Egan.

Jane remembered the leader bravely charging into the ring of horses, and she hit upon a plan. Very slowly she crawled back to Jim and climbed back in the saddle.

"Here goes nothin', Jim," she whispered into the horse's ear.

She spurred Jim and galloped through the trees, raising a whirlwind of dust and whooping wildly. When she reached the campsite, Jane fired off a volley of shots into the sky.

The warriors scattered as she skidded to a stop right beside the campfire, yelling and screaming and waving her bowie knife.

Jane shrieked, "Whoop, hi-ho, and cock-a-doodle-doo! I'm the original Missouri screamer. I was raised with rattlesnakes. I'm second cousin to a hurricane and first cousin to a seven-day blizzard. I'm so ferocious and ornery, it scares me to think about it! I'm tough as a bale of barbed wire and touchy as dynamite! Stand back, I'm going to let 'er rip!"

The warriors did not know what to make of this display of insanity—or was it courage? The woman was either out of her mind or had *wakan*—a special, strong power.

Jane jumped off of Jim. Egan couldn't understand what the scout was up to any more than the Sioux could. He signaled frantically for her to untie his bonds, but to his horror, Jane ignored him and pitched her pistol into the woods.

She unloaded several cans of beans from her saddlebags, then walked calmly over to the campfire and tossed on some extra wood.

As she cooked the beans, the Lakota braves approached. Jane saw wary curiosity in their dark eyes.

She nodded at the leader. "Howdy," she said, and offered her hand in greeting.

The leader returned her greeting, but she knew by his expression that he did not trust her.

"I'll need to borrow your pipe," Jane told Egan.

The captain looked just as puzzled as the Sioux.

Jane fished the items from his belt pouch, filled the pipe, and lit the tobacco with a long stick from the fire. She took a puff and passed it to Egan.

"What about you boys?" she asked the braves, repeating the offer in sign language.

The leader reached out slowly for the pipe. Normally the Lakotas made friends by sharing a peace pipe with a long stem and a red bowl. The leader handled Egan's short, curved pipe a little awkwardly and coughed a bit from the harsh tobacco. But he passed the pipe along to his neighbor, then took a long, hard look at Jane.

"Name's Jane," she said, signing as she spoke.

Jane would have laughed at the man's startled expression if she hadn't been afraid of offending him.

The leader turned and spoke rapidly to his companions. A

heavyset warrior stepped up to Jane and turned her head from side to side. It was Jane's turn to be startled when he laughed.

Jane scooped the beans into wooden bowls and passed them around. The heavyset warrior dug in eagerly, then frowned and swallowed with difficulty.

"I know they're bad," Jane signed. "But they're all I have."

The leader spoke to his men, and they took food from a large painted hide pouch. The leader introduced himself as Brave Hawk. His heavy companion was Likes to Sit. The tallest brave was Big Thunder.

Brave Hawk decided that Jane should be called Crazy Woman Who Cooks Bad Beans.

Jane signed to Brave Hawk that she didn't want to have to feed Captain Egan like a baby. The brave agreed to untie Egan's hands while they ate. But the captain's ankles remained tightly tied, and Jane noticed that the brave sitting closest to Egan never took his eyes off the captive.

Despite these precautions, Jane, Egan, and the braves enjoyed a feast around the fire.

"We ain't out of the woods yet, but jes' don't act scared," Jane whispered to Egan. "We may be able to slip off when they're asleep."

Jane signed to Brave Hawk. "Why is the blue coat a prisoner?"

Brave Hawk told Crazy Woman that the Lakotas had come to talk to the blue coats that morning but had been forced into fighting instead.

Jane muttered, "Darn that Tuttle!"

Brave Hawk decided Crazy Woman Who Cooks Bad Beans must have been sent by Nagi Tanka, the Sky Father. The Lakotas were very spiritual people who believed that nothing happened without a reason. Crazy Woman could talk to the blue coat chief. Brave Hawk hoped she had been sent to bring peace.

Brave Hawk signed to Crazy Woman, "Tell the blue coat chief we have no quarrel with him. We have hunted the settlers who entered the Paha Sapa, the sacred lands, seeking the yellow stones."

"What's he saying?" Egan demanded.

Jane said, "A pair of ornery claim jumpin' prospectors have been poking their shovels where they don't belong—up in the Black Hills. They're holed up in that cave."

"The men they were chasing?" Egan asked. "What are they going to do?"

Jane repeated Egan's questions in sign.

Brave Hawk told Jane the white men would be punished for their crimes. They had broken the treaty Red Cloud had made in Washington. The treaty promised the Lakotas the Paha Sapa for as long as the sky was blue and the grass was green.

Egan nodded when Jane had completed the translation. "That is the agreement. And tell him the United States Cavalry is here to protect the Sioux from trespassers. He should have come to us first."

Jane watched Brave Hawk's signs, then spoke. Her earlier guess had been correct. "The Lakotas were bringing the men to Fort Sanders, but Private Tuttle changed their minds," Jane explained. "They figured talking might get more of them killed."

Brave Hawk signed that the blue coats couldn't be trusted. He believed the words of Tatan'ka Iyota'ke, Sitting Bull, the great medicine man who lived near the Powder River. Sitting Bull said the settlers had thrown dust in Red Cloud's eyes when he made the treaty. The Lakotas would have no peace until they drove the settlers off their lands.

"Preserving the sacred lands is what the treaty's for," Jane signed. "And we'll keep that treaty!" she said, jumping to her feet.

Jane took a rope from Jim's saddle, then ran into the woods and found her Colt. She trotted back to Egan and asked, "You got any bullets?"

The captain sighed. He was used to giving the orders, but this situation was out of his hands. Egan's ankles ached from their bonds, and the wound in his thigh throbbed. He was in no shape to settle the conflict—and certainly didn't have the strength to argue with the determined woman standing over him. Jane's hand waited outstretched until the captain surrendered a handful of bullets.

"Thank you kindly." Jane bowed.

She loaded her Colt and marched to the mossy mouth of the cave. She fired a shot in the air.

"United States Cavalry!" Jane hollered in her deepest voice.

The braves stared at Crazy Woman Who Cooks Bad Beans. Was there no end to her madness?

The grubby dirt-caked prospectors rushed out. A scrawny man grabbed Jane's hand and grinned through stained yellow teeth. His foul breath blasted Jane as he said, "Man, are we glad to see you!"

"Woman," Jane corrected. "And you're under arrest." She pointed with the Colt and commanded, "Lay down there, and don't try anything funny."

Jane turned to Brave Hawk. She tossed the rope to him. He hog-tied the prospectors.

"Now these boys are gonna stand trial back at Fort Sanders," Jane told Brave Hawk. "The army has orders to keep prospectors off Sioux land."

Brave Hawk put Jim's bridle in Jane's hand. Big Thunder and Likes to Sit lifted the prospectors into their saddles.

"Don't you worry, boys. You'll get a fair trial before they hang you." Jane laughed. The prospectors groaned. "I'm just kidding you. They'll probably just make you eat army grub and build a railroad or something. Hard work's a tough prospect for someone who wants to get rich quick," Jane teased.

Captain Egan was astonished. Jane was the most unusual person—man or woman—he had ever met. She was a bit rough around the edges, but decent, fearless, foolish, and wise.

"You're quite a woman to have around in a calamity, Jane," Egan said.

"I like the sound of that," Jane mused. Then she slapped her thigh and grinned. "Calamity Jane!"

"Shall I call you that?" Egan asked.

"You can call me late for supper, so long as you don't fence me in," Calamity Jane said.

"This is a most improper request, and thoroughly against regulations, but I believe I'd like to keep you on as a scout," Egan said.

Jane shook her head. "Takin' orders just ain't the life for me. You won't have any more trouble from Brave Hawk here. He promised to see you back to the troop. I'd best be moving on now." Jane said, "Give my best to Siechrist, will you? And if you ever find Tuttle—shoot him for me."

She swung into Jim's worn saddle. "One more thing, Captain. Can you spare me any more bullets?"

The captain gave Jane a double handful of ammunition.

"Thank you kindly." Jane nodded. Then she pointed the black horse's strong neck into the sunset, toward the West, where a new land and new adventures waited.

She waved her hat in the air and whooped, "I'm Calamity Jane. Let 'er rip!"

EPILOG

Martha Jane Cannary, known as Calamity Jane, is one of the most colorful characters in frontier history. Her name is not remembered for any one spectacular achievement but rather because she embodied the bold, restless spirit of the West.

Born in Princeton, Missouri, in May 1852, Jane was the eldest of six children in the family of farmer Bob Cannary and his wife, Charlotte. At the end of the Civil War, the Cannary family moved to Salt Lake City, Utah, and later to Virginia City, Montana. Both parents died within a year of one another when Jane was fifteen years old.

Jane went on to work many different jobs, including bull train driver and waitress. She was a familiar face in many mining towns but spent most of her life in Deadwood, South Dakota, after that territory opened up in 1875.

In an age when women were expected to stay at home in whalebone corsets and floor-length gowns, Jane often dressed as a man and always did as she pleased. This habit alone was enough to make her notorious in stuffy nineteenth-century society.

In 1885, Jane married Clinton Burke, a one-legged Civil War veteran with a ten-year-old daughter. Together they ran a hotel in Boulder, Colorado, until they separated in 1901.

Calamity Jane loved to tell stories, especially outrageous ones about herself. She gave various reasons for her famous nickname, the rescue of Captain Egan being the most popular one.

Many of her tales of being an army scout, stagecoach driver, pony express rider, and other frontier adventures are probably exaggerations. By all accounts, she was a terrible shot and never killed anyone.

A legend in her own lifetime, Jane was the heroine of countless dime novels and even the subject of a play. She also appeared briefly in Buffalo Bill Cody's Wild West Show.

Calamity Jane felt a sentimental devotion to Wild Bill Hickok, the legendary lawman and scout who was the hero of even more dime novels than Jane. Although Bill's friends deny the connection, Jane often told stories about her romance with Wild Bill. Her last words were, "Bury me next to Wild Bill." And in 1903, Jane was buried twenty feet from her beloved idol in Mount Moriah Cemetery in Deadwood.